WARNING

This book contains sexually explicit scenes and adult language. It may be considered offensive to some readers. This book is for sale to adults ONLY.

* * * * * * * * * * * * * * * * *

Please store your files wisely where they cannot be accessed by underage readers.

ISBN-13: 978-1987863970
ISBN-10: 1987863976

Other Books by Darla Dunbar:

<u>The Romeo Alpha BBW Paranormal Shifter Romance Series</u>

Amanda Walker thinks that she has a normal and boring life. That is until after her 24th birthday. Everything changes when she meets the man who says he was supposed to be her husband. Denying everything the man says, she fights him every step of the way. But after he kidnaps her, Amanda discovers that there are some things about her family that her parents kept a secret all these years. Among the history of the family she learns secrets she thought only happened in story books. Can Amanda tell the difference between truth and lies or is she this mysterious woman that holds the key to a legacy?

<u>Romeo Alpha Blood Lines Romance Series</u>

Twenty-four years have passed in relative peace for Amanda and Romeo. They've raised five children into adulthood and are thoroughly enjoying their lives as the Alpha King and Queen of the werewolves. At twenty-four, Sarina is just stepping into her powers and will be ripe for mating when her birthday comes in two weeks. What no one knows is the danger that lurks just outside their tight knit community. Romeo has made peace with the other clans and has enjoyed that peace, but it will all come crashing down around him when his oldest daughter comes of age to take a mate.

The Alpha Feud BBW Paranormal Shifter Romance Series

Eliza's life consisted of reporting on boring, crowd-pleasing events, like their country livestock fair. With the arrival of two handsome brothers, the lives of Eliza and her best friend, Melissa, are shaken to the core. For Eliza, the arrival of this new man becomes a test of her relationship with her current boyfriend, who she's been happily living with for over six years. Does Hayden, a complete stranger, really wield the power to make Eliza reconsider her relationship with Andrew?

The Alpha Packed BBW Paranormal Shifter Romance Series

Darlene has led a quiet life since suffering through a terrible break-up. She wants nothing more than to spend her time in front of the TV, away from any sort of trouble. But all that goes down the drain when handsome, rugged and rough Idris comes into her life. He is a werewolf on the lookout for his missing pack leader. Darlene quickly finds herself pulled towards this mysterious man and at the same time finds herself falling deeper and deeper into the world of the supernatural.

The Daemon Paranormal Romance Chronicles

The daemon infighting can only be stopped when a strong leader emerges to calm the different factions. Juno appears to be at the heart of the conflict. Things become complicated when Phoebe and Supay try to negotiate with the siren, Juno. The love triangle among Phoebe, Supay and Apollo become tense when Juno's meddling threatens to destroy any romance that develops.

<u>The Leather Satchel Paranormal Romance Series</u>

Valtina is stuck in Middle World, unable to pass on to The Afterlife. In order to redeem herself from past deeds done, she must help bring romance back into the world and stop The Dark Side from destroying love in its entirety. Following orders issued by Ladaya and armed with a leather satchel filled with the appropriate tools and weapons, Valtina embraces each mission with enthusiasm.

Get the latest update on new releases from the author at:

https://darladunbar.com/newsletter/

This book is Part Two of the "The Mind Talker Paranormal Romance Series"

Book 1 - Awareness

Ananda discovered that she can read other people's mind when she was 11. It is supposed to be a gift but it's driving her crazy. Lonely and disoriented, Ananda runs off to New York. She thinks that in a city as big as that, there must be someone like her walking around. One day, man's voice calls out to her. The strange thing is that she heard the voice in her mind.

Book 2 - Hunted

Jared's past haunted him and served as a reminder that he can't escape his fate. If he had stopped the boy back then, would his sister still be alive? Jenny was the love of Jared's life until he discovered she was living a double life. Jenny was part of a secret organization that was bent on hunting him.

Book 3 - Heat

Ananda couldn't help herself. Jared's scent just sends her over the edge. No one else understood Ananda's gift... not even her parents. When Jared found Ananda, he explained what her special powers meant. Only certain people acquired the gift of reading minds. Along with that, Ananda was undergoing a maturation process. Every one of her kind will experience it in their 21st year.

Book 4 - Revealed

Jared learns the truth about his dead sister. Ananda had
the power to see into his past. She saw what he saw
during that fateful day when Jared's sister died.
Meanwhile, the truth about Kerri's family is revealed.
They are the sole reason why Ananda and her kind are
on the endangered list.

Book 5 - Evasion

Ryan is the mystery man who is helping Jared and
Ananda to escape to Canada in hopes of evading the
organization that is hunting all those with special mind
reading powers. Kerri's family is behind the secret
organization. Her love for Ryan has forced her to
choose between loyalty to family and loyalty to Ryan.
Can she be trusted?

The Mind Talker Paranormal Romance Series

Hunted

Book Two

By Darla Dunbar

Copyright Revelry Publishing 2015

Table of Contents

Chapter One

WAKING UP was an experience for Jared. It had been years since he had felt an inkling of the comfort that is sleeping wrapped around someone he didn't have to worry about stabbing him in the back. It had been months since he last let his guard down enough to be intimate with anyone other than himself. And yet this girl, someone who had never even been properly informed of what she was, had somehow blown clear past all of his defenses before he even realized they were down. It gave him an uneasy feeling the fact that he responded to her so quickly. He had thought himself incapable of feeling anything for another person other than hate and mistrust after all he had been through.

Jared's life wasn't rough in the beginning. He grew up in a normal family household, with normal parents, a normal older sister and a normal dog. Overall his early life was completely and utterly normal. And then came puberty.

His freshman year of high school brought the normal bouts of acne and anger indicative of a boy on the journey of becoming a man. Being the nerd that he originally was, he had read every article and book on the subject that he could get his grubby little hands on, including some not so hidden Playboys that his dad kept stashed in a cooler in the garage. Everything that he had been experiencing was so tragically normal that it was almost a relief when he started hearing the voices. At first he had thought himself crazy, mad like the hatter from Alice and Wonderland, until the voices began to sound familiar. He could make out his sister's voice, shrill and lively even when muted. Then it was his parents. Soon he was hearing every thought contained in his high school and he realized what real crazy was.

It was a chilly day in November, the day before Thanksgiving break, ironically, when one of his classmates, a boy who had been picked on and bullied for years and who Jared had been close acquaintances with moving in similar social circles, decided that he couldn't handle the pressure anymore. Jared had known that the boy, Kevin, was unstable just by listening to his rather disturbing thoughts day in and day out. He could hear the boy plotting something big, something that would stop his never-ending pain. Jared had known all this and yet he had done nothing. He was still getting a handle on control and though the boy's thoughts were filled with darkness, on the outside he appeared put together and in control. Jared feared that at best no one would believe him and at worst he'd put himself in harm's way if Kevin decided to take out his anger on him. So Jared stayed quiet, never even telling his sister who was in the year above him, his concerns.

Jared had been sitting out on the lacrosse field where he normally took his lunch so he could avoid any awkwardness in the school cafeteria. His sister had often offered him a seat with her friends, but he usually turned her down in favor of his solo spot. It wasn't that he was anti-social, it was just that he knew one day he would grow into his looks and be, if not attractive, then at least average. However, he didn't want to sit for forty-five minutes and hear his sister's harpy friends with their high-pitched inner voices squawking and gushing over it. He thought that people who said women mature faster than men were horribly misinformed and probably home-schooled.

It was for this very reason that Jared heard rather than saw the commotion that happened without any warning. One minute he was biting into an apple, geometry book balanced on one knee, and the next he found himself sprawled on his side with his ears ringing as his lungs fought to pull in air. All around he could see bits of rock and drywall lying beside him and for one minute he wondered if he was dreaming. Slowly he started to make out the sounds of screams over his groans as he pushed his body up into a seated position. The scene that unfolded before him was straight out of a war movie. The school was entirely engulfed by flames and one of the cafeteria walls was completely missing. Some students were running out of side entrances while others were already huddled across the street, loudly wailing and clutching one another for comfort. All around Jared could hear the flood of thoughts running wild.

"Oh my God! It's just like in a movie!"

"What's happening?"

"My classmates are dead. I saw a dead body…oh God, I saw a dead body!"

Covering his ears to try to block out the voices, Jared stood in an attempt to get as far away from the building as possible until he heard the one voice he had always been careful to block out.

"Jared…safe…hurts…"

"Sofie!" The sound of his sister's inner voice, so weak and in pain sparked Jared into action. He moved to go towards the cafeteria, into the area where he knew his sister always sat when four strong arms grabbed him and pulled him away from the scene. Screaming and yelling, he fought to free himself and free his sister from the crumbling debris, but the hands were too strong for him. Soon all he could do was shake as he stood across the road and watched firefighters and emergency officers fighting to put out the blaze. Some students were being carried out in stretchers or on the backs of others. Jared watched closely, desperately hoping to see his sister's long midnight black hair among those being brought over. He watched until the blaze was out and emergency workers began searching for bodies. He watched until his parents pulled up, his mother screaming and beating the chest of the officer appointed to the task of delivering the bad news. He watched his father slump to the ground, head clutched in his meaty hands as he sobbed for the first time Jared had ever seen. He watched it all and he knew.

This was all his fault.

His sister's death was one of many that day. Out of the three-hundred students in the cafeteria that day only twenty managed to make it out alive. Kevin had apparently made the decision to take out his tormenters as well as himself and had situated himself as close to that table as possible before detonating his bomb, a bomb he had strapped to himself and had hidden under his clothes. The official report was that the boy had been planning this for a long while and had found instructions on the internet for how to build a bomb out of normal every day materials. It also had a quote from Kevin's mother stating that her son had been harassed for years by his classmates and that he had recently began 'hearing voices.' That last statement stopped Jared cold. It was then that he realized the deaths of over two hundred of his classmates was and would forever be on his conscience. If only he had stopped and talked to Kevin, let him know he wasn't alone in the world of voices then maybe this tragedy never would have occurred. Maybe they could have learned to help each other and maybe Sofie would still be alive to pester Jared into dressing better or telling him how handsome he would be when he got older. Maybe she wouldn't be rotting in the ground while their parents' marriage fell apart. Her death meant the death of their family and the beginning of their father's love of alcohol. Jared retreated even further into himself, switching schools when his mother moved them across town and making minimal effort to get to know anyone. He graduated with honors, moved across country to attend Columbia, and as Sofie and her friends predicted, he grew very well into his looks. Working out 5-6 times a week gave him the relief he needed by pushing his body until the point of exhaustion. The fortuitous side effect of such hard work was an impressive physique. Suddenly he went from a nobody to a somebody that girls and guys alike wanted to sleep with.

Chapter Two

He had been frequenting the library looking for books and articles about people exhibiting extra abilities when he really should have been working on his literature paper when he first met Jenny. Unlike some of the girls he had previously gone for, she seemed to be more mature and put together. Her thoughts were a gentle hum in his mind rather than the chaotic ramblings he was privy to when interacting with other girls on campus. He could only really catch a word or maybe an errant feeling and rather than being wary of that, he was intrigued. It had been a long time since he found anyone out of the ordinary and he was curious to learn more about her.

It had taken him weeks to get her to actually talk to him thanks to his impressive reputation around campus for being a 'one and done' type of guy. However, once they began talking he discovered that they had quite a bit in common. She was double majoring in neuroscience and pre-law and believed that the next step of evolution would not be one of physical means but rather mental. Her ideas of the next step of evolution were fascinating to Jared and he wondered if perhaps she had abilities of her own. Then came the day she finally let down her defenses and it happened.

They had been having an invigorating discussion on what would be the next step after the discovery of evolved humans when Jared leaned across the couch and kissed Jenny. Initially she didn't respond and Jared began to worry that he had misread the situation, until the moment he felt her fingers tangle in his hair angling his head so that their lips slotted together perfectly. The moment their tongues touched he knew that he wouldn't be sleeping around with anyone else. Something about her called to him and his body responded faster than it ever had before. Before long he was straining uncomfortably in his jeans and he could feel the fabric beginning to soak through thanks to his weeping member. Making an executive decision, Jared hooked his hands under Jenny's knees and stood up. She wrapped her legs around his waist as he carried her into the single bedroom in his apartment.

Laying her down and removing himself from her warmth was a test in patience and they both laughed at the clumsiness of their hands as they quickly stripped one another of all clothing. Once Jenny had him stripped, she moved faster than he thought she could until all he could feel was the pleasurable warmth of her sinfully wicked mouth.

"God Jenny, your mouth," he groaned, fingers tracing the edge of her mouth where it met his pulsing cock. What little she couldn't fit into her mouth was being squeezed and massaged by her small but confident hands. Jared could feel tremors running up and down his spine as he fought not to let go too quickly. He could feel every ridge on the roof of her mouth as her head bobbed torturously slowly up and down his shaft. The slurping sounds alone nearly made Jared lose his head as he stared at Jenny's hollowed out cheeks. He could see saliva and his own slick dripping steadily down the girl's chin as she made humming noises to express her enjoyment. The vibrations set off nerve endings and had fireworks appearing in front of Jared's eyes until he forced himself to pull Jenny up in order to chase the taste of his own wetness from the heat of her mouth.

Jenny broke the kiss with a moan and pushed Jared to lay flat on the bed. "Lie back and relax baby." She positioned herself about Jared's lap, her moist core dangerously close to his uncovered cock. Jared had never slept with anyone without some form of contraception and for some reason unknown to him he felt no desire to push the issue. He already knew he'd be with this woman until she pushed him away and so he was ready to take whatever she wanted to give.

The feeling of her moist heated walls against the skin of his shaft was damn near overwhelming and Jared could do little more than grip the sheet with one hand and Jenny's hip with the other.

"Jared baby, you feel so good." Jenny rocked slowly up and down only pulling off slightly before re-seating herself firmly with a little swivel in her hip. "Feel me up so nice. Your big hard cock pushing inside of me."

Jared groaned, the sound of sweet Jenny talking dirty to him was enough to push him right back to that edge. "Fuck Jen. Too good I'm gonna shoot already."

"Then maybe we should slow down, do something else?" Jenny abruptly moved off Jared and laid on her back beside him with her knees pointed out. "Maybe I want a little of that oral pleasure, hmm?"

"Oh yeah Jen?" Jared quickly flipped over and slid down so that his hips were under Jenny's thighs. "You want me to taste you, drink you until you've got nothing left to give?" Using a finger, Jared traced up and down the woman's sensitive folds, smiling at the shiver that ran down her body. He could see her shiny hole already slightly wider thanks to his cock having been in there only moments before. Moving his face closer, Jared breathed in deep and was startled to find that Jenny didn't smell like much of anything down there. It wasn't good or bad, just completely non-existent. He wasn't sure what that was supposed to mean as he didn't usually offer this to any of his female partners, but he did think that women were supposed to have a certain kind of smell. When Jenny moaned though and her body pumped out a bit more slick, all thoughts of the strangeness left Jared and he was once again focused on the gorgeous writhing creature before him.

Putting his lips to her folds, Jared let his tongue dart out and push slowly into her hidden depths. Her taste was a bit like her scent in that it was barely there or non-existent. Still, he wanted to try hard to make it good for her. He opened her carefully with his fingers while flicking his tongue rapidly in an obscene parody of what his still hard cock wanted to do to her. He could hear soft gasps and moans leaking from her mouth and he reveled in being able to make her feel overcome with pleasure. Before long he could feel a subtle shift in her body before her walls contracted and she was flung headfirst into ecstasy.

Jared slowly withdrew his tongue and leaned up to cover Jenny's body with his own. When he tried to kiss her, she was quick to turn her head however, and didn't seem interested in tasting herself on Jared's lips. He chalked it up to personal preference before reaching down to slide himself in deep. He could feel their hips meet and he paused to enjoy the silkiness of her channel. Soon though nature made him move as his instinct to bury himself in her took control. The sound of skin slapping together was almost deafening, Jenny throwing her head back to voice her pleasure to the world as Jared buried his grunts and groans into the dampness of her neck. Her nails scratched lines on his shoulder blades and that little bit of pain is what sent him tumbling over the edge, hips speeding up as his body pumped his release into Jenny's moist cavern. Both of them were panting and out of breath, loathe to move and break the afterglow of their first coupling. Soon enough Jared disentangled himself from the bed and moved to the bathroom to get a wet cloth in order to clean them up. He tried not to think too hard after seeing his release leaking down Jenny's thighs and instead curled up beside the already dozing woman.

The next few weeks were nothing short of amazing for Jared. He had a woman who was beautiful, intelligent and loved having sex whenever and wherever the mood struck her. She had once cornered him in a section of the library that was seldom frequented in order to suck him off. One minute Jared was laughing and playing along and the next he was stuffing a fist in his mouth to keep from shouting the place down as Jenny showed that she had mastered the art of deepthroating. The force with which he came was terrifyingly amazing and his brain was so shot he didn't notice that Jenny hadn't swallowed but instead had spit into a jar.

Then there was the time Jenny had handcuffed him to the bed, put a bandana over his eyes and then ridden Jared for close to an hour. Every time Jenny could feel him getting close she would stop moving, instead just holding Jared's hard member inside of her. He felt a little uncomfortable at first with the idea of being tied down and blinded, but he pushed away the feeling and concentrated on pushing himself to climax. During this time he could never quite get a read on Jenny's thoughts. He could feel that she was pleased with herself but it was still mostly silence from her thoughts. If he hadn't been so enamored of her, maybe he would have taken the time to wonder about the silence he got from her mind; how someone without abilities was able to shield herself from him with little to no effort. But he was in love and he thought those feelings were reciprocated until the day came that pushed him onto the path of searching for people like him and running from those who hunted him.

"Jen I don't think this is a good idea," Jared whispered as he ducked under a wooden beam. He was clutching a flashlight as he followed Jenny into an abandoned building. He wasn't completely sure how she convinced him to sneak into the building. It was only that Jenny had told him she wanted to explore the old asylum because of its history of inhumane treatments. She wanted to see if she could find any files that detailed the happenings.

"Don't worry! This place has been abandoned for decades now. No one is going to come in and kick us out or anything." Jenny stopped and leaned heavily against Jared's side, fingertips trailing down his chest and toying with the edge of his jeans. Just that little motion caused a flare of heat to rush through his body and he knew his cheeks must be slightly tinted pink with his arousal. For the past few months his arousal had been hitting hard and heavy to the point that he swore he could actually smell his body releasing citrusy smelling pheromones. He wondered if Jenny could smell them as she never commented or even seemed to be aware of it.

"I'm not worried about that," Jared lied easily. "It just doesn't seem like this place is all that safe and I don't want you to get hurt…" Feeling slightly foolish, Jared let his voice trail off into silence and continued to follow Jenny deeper into the building while alarm bells went off in his head. Something just wasn't right about what they were doing.

"Jen seriously, I don't think we should be doing this." Jared glanced around the darkened room, eyes straining against what meager light they had to see if anything was out of place.

"You're right about that, but it's too late for you now." Suddenly pain bloomed hot and bright across

Jared's temple as the world went pitch black around him.

When Jared awoke, he was chained against the wall and he could feel blood dripping down his scalp. He was startled to see Jenny sitting calmly in front of him, not a scratch on her but with a smirk he had never seen her wear before.

"Jen?"

"Not quite love." Standing, the woman who had been his lover for the past six months looked at him with barely contained triumph and disgust. With a jolt Jared realized that all of the moments they spent together, all of the memories and future plans had been nothing but lies. He should have questioned himself harder as to why he couldn't hear Jenny's thoughts. Why all he had ever gotten were vague emotions and sporadic words. Why after all of the time he had spent in the library he had never seen her there before the day they met. His blind, naïve trust had made him an easy catch and what's more, he had willingly run headlong into it with his desire to be loved. He could feel something within him hardening and he knew then that feelings of love and devotion were nothing more than a weakness, a tool others could use against you to get what they want.

"Who are you?" Jared asked, none of the traces of who he used to be evident in his voice. He felt a sick thrill when the smirk on the woman's face slipped just a little. He could almost smell the nervousness starting to radiate from her. "Why did you bring me here? Why play this sick game with me?" His voice rising, Jared could feel a tickle starting at the base of his skull. It was almost like an insistent itch that he longed to scratch. Jenny's smirk fell completely and she was left looking distinctly unprepared for the questions Jared was asking. Her confusion only fueled Jared's rage and heaved himself off the floor to stand fully in front of her. "Answer my fucking questions!"

Rather than surprise her, his command seemed to relax the woman whose face went from surprise to blank as if she were unaware of herself.

"My name is Jodie Hamilton." Her voice was almost monotone, devoid of any inflection. Jared stared for a moment, mystified by the sudden change in the woman's demeanor.

"Good. Why did you bring me here?" Arms straining, Jared fought to break the handcuffs that bound him to the wall while keeping his eyes locked on the woman in front of him.

"I brought you for my boss. He ordered you to be contained in a secure location until his arrival." The information was making Jared's head spin. From what it sounded like, his seduction and abduction had been premeditated before he and Jenny had ever met. It might even be possible that her whole reason for even coming to the college was to find Jared and set him up. The memories of them spending so many nights twined together in the throes of what Jared had thought was mutual passion made him want to vomit.

Looking up at the woman who had lied to him for months gave Jared the strength and sheer anger to not break down. "Who is your boss? What does he want with me?"

"I don't know. He never shares that much information with me. I'm supposed to find you, seduce you and deliver you to the drop off point for extraction." Jared could see Jenny's body beginning to shake as if she were trying to fight off whatever hold he had on her. What little light her lamp provided showed that her skin was ashen gray and dotted with beads of sweat. He knew he needed to push hard and fast if he wanted to get out before whatever Calvary she had called actually arrived.

"Fine," Jared all but growled, irritated by the skin of his wrists as the cuffs bit into them. Eyes snapping up to Jenny's, he summoned every bit of a commanding tone he could scrounge. "Uncuff me." He could see Jenny's hand snap up and then hesitate as if she were unsure whether or not that was a good idea. His eyes narrowed in fury as what little patience he had ran out. "NOW!"

To his surprise and amazement, Jenny hurried to fulfill his command, bringing out the keys and unlocking his handcuffs. The moment Jared was free he grabbed the woman by the back of the neck, barely able to contain his fury as he stared into the eyes of the woman he thought he would one day marry.

"I want you to forget you ever met me. Forget you were ever supposed to find me. Leave this building and never think of me again." Jared reluctantly let go and watched as Jenny turned and left the room. That was the last time he dared to imagine himself having a normal life.

Chapter Three

In the months and years after, Jared practiced using his newfound gift of persuasion. He still had numerous liaisons with women, but now he made sure that they would forget him after, and he was always careful to use protection. He switched his major to computer science and began studying and honing skills he needed to obtain information on who or what might be hunting him and others like him. It was completely by accident that he had run into Ananda a few months ago. The minute he felt her mind touch his it was as if time itself stopped. Not even with Jenny had he ever felt this way and the idea of an even greater loss of control with another person made him wish for some harm to befall the girl. She looked to be a few years younger than him with thick wavy auburn hair and striking golden eyes. A trick of the light almost made her eyes seem to glow with a fire that threatened to scorch him. And as if all of those things hadn't been attractive enough, there was her scent, honey sweet and trailing behind her as if by command. She seemed to be completely unaware of the eyes that were drawn to her in her wake as she laughed with a smaller waif-like girl with blazing red hair and eyes that seemed to swirl with magic. It was worrying that all he could get from the smaller girl was a faint hum and a feeling of contentment, but he ignored the tightening of his chest in favor of moving along down his path.

Despite his desire to ignore the girl, he found himself growing more and more intrigued. Who was she? Did she know about her abilities? Did her friend know? All these questions and more were running through his brain and he pledged to find answers to them. It was scarily easy to obtain information about her from the registrar. He knew that her name was Ananda Reyes and that she lived in the student apartments just on the edge of campus with the red-headed girl. He knew she was aware of her abilities and he'd seen her use them in ways that were eerily similar to his own.

He told himself that he was just looking out for her in a brotherly way, making sure she didn't get into too much trouble. And yet every time he saw her go home with some boy who wasn't him, a part of him burned bright with rage. It wasn't until the moment that he was pressed against her in the alley that he realized just how far he had fallen. The sight of his old lover, Jenny, walking into that apartment had spurred him into action. With Ananda unaware of what awaited her immediate future, Jared knew his fate was sealed. He would go to the ends of the Earth and back just to make sure this girl was safe.

Though he had pledged to himself to keep Ananda safe, he was unprepared for the effect her scent would have on him. He found himself hardening fast, and even though they were surrounded by the stench of trash and waste, the desire to bend her over and have her right then and there was damn near overwhelming. Only the thought of being caught by whoever had been hunting him kept him from doing something incredibly stupid in the alley. No, he will save it for later.

In retrospect, being contained in a small space with the object of your desire spilling fresh pheromones everywhere probably wasn't the best idea he had ever had. If he had been a better man, he would have gotten two separate rooms and retreated to take care of his sexual frustration alone. He may have been able to control himself if not for the innocent thought that drifted his way.

"Why do you smell so good?"

The realization that Ananda could smell him as much as he could smell her broke whatever control Jared thought he had and before he could regain his senses he found himself balls deep, buried in a warmth that threatened to break the tenuous hold he had on his feelings. Every thrust felt like a cleansing and every gasp and moan like the words of an angel. Afterwards as he lay beside her sleeping body, Jared's eyes took in everything about her from the point of her nose to the ample swelling of her bosom. Somehow in the midst of so much chaos and pain, he had managed to find the woman who would complete him. He didn't know how he knew, but he just knew. And now that he had her wrapped safely in his arms, he dared anyone to try to come and rip them apart.

He knew that this battle wasn't over; it hadn't even truly begun. For some reason there were people out there hunting people like him and Ananda, and Jared would not rest until he could be sure that the woman asleep in his arms would be safe.

To be continued in Book 3

If you enjoyed this title, I would appreciate your leaving a review of the book. Good reviews encourage an author to write as well as help books to sell. Good reviews can be just a few short sentences describing what you liked about the book without having a spoiler. If you could spend 30 seconds writing a review, I would appreciate it: you can review this title right now at your favorite retailer.

Here is a preview of the **next story** you may enjoy:

Heat - The Mind Talker Paranormal Romance Series, Book 3

TYPICALLY, on a normal day, Ananda woke up securely warm and cocooned in the down-filled blankets of her bed. The window over her bed had no blinds, only sheer curtains that fully allowed the rising sun to shine brightly, illuminating the room and waking her gradually. What she did not normally wake up to is her skin overwrought with sensitive nerves, itchiness demanding her attention, and skin feeling one degree away from boiling. Slitting her eyes open, Ananda could see moonlight seeping through a crack in curtains that absolutely did not belong to her, creating random shadow patterns on the wall that did nothing to calm the frantic beating of her heart. If not for the familiar arm stretched out around her waist, she would have jerked out of bed. As it was she simply gazed around while letting her mind catch up to the situation.

Shifting slightly, Ananda was unpleasantly surprised when a bolt of pain shot down her spine. "Ow ow, fuck ow! What the hell did you do to me?!"

"…Nothing that you didn't ask for."

The unexpected answer pushed a small huff of laughter between Ananda's lips until her breath was coming out in wheezing gasps. She could feel herself beginning to panic and who could blame her? Her skin felt like it was on fire, she was in bed with a man she met barely a day ago and she was running from some unknown entity that broke into the house she shared with a best friend who she was afraid she'd either never see again or would only hear about on the news. All things considered, panicking was the tamest thing she could be doing at this point when compared to the alternatives such as running screaming into oncoming traffic.

Ananda considered calling her parents and then quickly pushed that thought from her mind. All she needed was for them to once again think that she was crazy when she explained about hearing other people's voices and apparently finding someone who shared that same gift. Not to mention having to explain to them that she was currently shacked up with said person in a slightly sleazy hotel room after having explosive sex that left her catatonic for…

"How long have I been out?" Ananda would have been surprised by the breathy quality of her voice if she weren't still trying to gain control of her body and regulate her breathing. The hand that had been resting on her stomach was now moving softly in a circle that, amazingly, was helping her regain her sense of calm. That musky, citrusy scent was back and curling softly about her, somehow cooling the heat that settled right underneath her skin. She could feel the aches from their previous bedroom activities diminishing until all she felt was a dull buzz. "God that's like catnip or something…" Her voice trailed off into a satisfied gasp. The hand on her stomach paused for a moment but once again continued after she whimpered softly.

If you enjoyed this sample then look for **Heat - The Mind Talker Paranormal Romance Series, Book 3**.

Here is a preview of **another story** you may enjoy:

WALKING OUT of the hotel room, Phoebe jumped
back in surprise. Her dog, Ace, ran up to her. "Ace!
What are you doing here?" She leaned down to pet him.
"Come inside with me and we will get you something
to eat."

Bringing him inside with her, she glanced over at
Apollo. She met his questioning eyes with a shrug. "I
have no clue how he got here. It seems impossible, but
here he is."

Apollo shrugged. "Weirder things have happened. I
guess we can just bring him along with us. Having him
could help." Standing up, he grabbed the bag of
weapons and restraints. Together, they left the room
and got in the car.

Parking near the jade shop, the pair sipped coffee as
they waited for Qilin to close the shop. They inched the
car along behind her as she went to a park. The sunlight
was quickly fading away and few people were in the
park. Quickly, they got out of the car and followed
Qilin into a clearing. Although they walked in absolute
silence, Qilin turned around.

"I knew you were there. This is your last chance to
turn back. Are you ready?" She widened her stance and
stood confidently in front of them. Phoebe stepped back
so that Apollo could do what he came for.

Grabbing a dagger out of the bag, Apollo nodded. "I
am ready if you are." As soon as he finished the

sentence, Qilin became a blazing ball of fire. Flames radiated from her arms and curled into balls within her hands. Throwing the fire at Apollo, she moved forward. Apollo ducked the flames and tried to get into an offensive position.

Ace whined next to Phoebe. Leaning down, she patted his head reassuringly. In reality, she was shaking in fear. Still unused to the world of daemons, the fiery daemon before her was a frightening surprise. She felt less terrible about the possibility of Qilin's death. The daemon before her was far from defenseless. Before this moment, how many other potential leaders had tried to kill Qilin and failed?

Qilin threw another ball of fire and it singed Apollo's heels. The grass in the clearing was quickly becoming torched by their fight. Ball after ball of fire was thrown and Apollo managed to shrug it off without any difficulties. Unfortunately, he was unable to stand long enough to get close to her. It was too late when he realized that he should have just used a gun. Rolling away from another ball of fire, he quickly darted in the opposite direction. The sudden change of direction surprised Qilin, and she let the ball of fire go too soon. It released from her hand and flew directly toward Phoebe. Apollo either did not notice where the fire was headed or did not care. He adjusted his stance and lifted the dagger behind his head to throw it.

If you enjoyed this sample then look for **The Shifter - The Daemon Paranormal Romance Chronicles, Book 2.**

Here is a preview of **another story** you may enjoy:

Alpha Packed: A BBW Paranormal Shifter Romance - Book 2

AT FIRST there was only the hunger. It pulsed through Rebecca, tricking her into thinking she was actually alive. But she knew better than that, didn't she? She spent most of the night staring into a mirror, seeing nothing in the reflection… as if she had been wiped from the pages of the history books completely.

They were looking for her. She saw posters plastered around town, asking for any information on where she had gone since the bookshop was ransacked. She kept her head low and chopped off most of her hair in exchange for the semblance of a normal hairstyle. She had gone back to try and find her friend, Darlene.

But the hunger clouded everything. It was too dangerous to talk to anyone. Then it became too dangerous to even stand near them. The smell of their skin, alive, with blood pumping just under the surface, was too much to bear. She had retreated into the woods.

Just as daylight approached, she stumbled across an empty cabin that overlooked the highway. Clawing at the floorboards, she managed to get herself into the ground before the sunlight could shine into the cabin.

Now it was the middle of the night and she was staring at the soulless mirror. She was almost glad she couldn't see herself. She didn't want to see herself. Because the mess behind her was already too gruesome. A hitchhiker had thought she could stay here the night as well…but she was fatally mistaken.

No, Rebecca didn't want to see herself in the mirror. She didn't need to, because she knew what the mirror would show. Her face, smeared red... her hands, coated in the hitchhiker's blood. Rebecca could just make out the girl's hand, sticking out from behind the makeshift bed, her fingers curled slightly, a slick pool of blood sliding out from underneath her body. It was her first feeding and she made a huge mess of it.

Rebecca closed her eyes and screamed.

"Am I under suspicion of anything?"

"No, ma'am."

"Truly? Because it honestly feels like you suspect me of something." Darlene crossed her arms and leaned back in the chair, staring down Officer Walsh. Normally, she had the utmost respect for police officers and knew Walsh was just doing his job. But she couldn't help but think of him as a pain in the ass.

"Listen, Miss Troop, I'm just trying to understand why you went to see Ms. Boots that night."

"And I told you a thousand times already. I tried to make you guys aware of the forum post by her son that I found. I was blown off here, so I went to his mother directly to tell her."

"I just don't understand why you're involved in an old case from someone who has no connection with you whatsoever."

"Why does it matter? I didn't murder her, and it feels like you're suggesting I did. Do I need to get a lawyer?"

Walsh paled. "No, there's no need for that, ma'am. They're just routine questions. What did Ms. Boots say when you went to her with your information?"

"She told me she had known already that he thought he was a werewolf. She told me that he fell in with the wrong crowd. She was very sad about it all. But she confirmed that someone picked Brent up that night. So my information was useless, like the cops said. Brent's mother already knew that someone came for him that night."

Darlene hoped her story sounded convincing. Most of the details were true. It was just the circumstances of the details that were fudged a little.

Walsh looked down at his notepad. "What about *Roman's Tavern*? Witnesses put you there last week. Your boyfriend got into a fight with Roman. No cops were called, and the two of you bailed afterward, from my understanding."

Darlene's heart thrummed. For a second, she wanted to shake Idris. Why in the world did he fight with Roman that night? Of course people would have seen them and word would have gotten back to the police. It was a vicious fight. She didn't know that Walsh had heard about the fight already though. Who blabbed?

"So?"

"So if Roman decides to press charges, your boyfriend will be in a lot of trouble."

"As far as I know, Roman didn't press charges. So what is the question?"

"Why were you at *Roman's Tavern* that night?"

"I can't go to a bar with my boyfriend?"

Walsh leaned forward. "I just find it strange that after I mentioned to you that Jacob was interested in going to *Roman's Tavern* that you ended there as well. And you seemed so interested in Brent Boot's death, that he had a connection to *Roman's Tavern* as well."

Darlene felt warm. She didn't like lying to the police. But it wasn't as if they would believe the truth anyway. *Well, the truth is, my boyfriend is a werewolf. His pack leader wanted to exile himself from the werewolves in order to craft a werewolf-vampire hybrid creature. No, don't worry – he's dead! Yeah, I killed him with the help of a spirit. Yes, I said spirit. Turns out, I have power over ghosts that no one understands, myself included. Jacob is a hybrid and is out there somewhere doing God only knows what. My best friend is a missing vampire, and her Maker is a crazy bitch. You are chasing leads that go nowhere because my insane social circle, including my werewolf Exsul boss, is on the case!*

Ugh. It sounded like a terrible anime.

"This is just a questioning, right?" When Walsh nodded, Darlene stood up. "Then I'm done for the day.

I have to get to work. The bookstore re-opens tomorrow. Where are you on my missing friend, by the way… while you sit here and accuse me of murder?"

"No one is accusing you of anything, Miss Troop. We don't have any leads on your friend yet. Has she been in touch with you?"

"No," Darlene said, trying to keep the sadness out of her voice. "I'm leaving now."

Walsh shook his head as Darlene left the room. It felt as if every cell in her body was vibrating slightly, making her head hurt. She dreaded this police station now. Why did she ever try to tell them about Brent and his forum post? It just ended up biting her in the ass.

As she stepped out into the sunlight and slid a pair of sunglasses on, she thought of Rebecca. Still no sign of her. Darlene was hoping Rebecca would try to call her. She kept thinking back to Rebecca opening her eyes and bursting out of the room, into the night. Guilt immersed heavily in her heart. Idris warned her that newborn vampires were feral and dangerous. Usually their Makers remained nearby to help guide them through their ordeal. But Vivica had no interest in taking care of Rebecca.

Darlene got in her car, ignoring whispers from a couple of teenagers nearby. She knew they were talking about her negatively, making remarks on her weight. *I don't care. I'm above this shit.* If she repeated it enough times, maybe it would finally sink in.

She looked at her phone and saw a text from Idris. He asked how the meeting with Walsh went. Darlene paused, unsure of what to type. She was touched that he had texted her with everything else going on in his world. *My boyfriend.* The phrase seemed so foreign to her. How could Idris, such an imposing, strong and sexy werewolf, be dating her, of all people?

Darlene lectured herself again. She deserved this. She deserved to have a boyfriend who made her happy, was great in bed and clearly interested in her. She had to stop trying to ruin herself and not let herself be happy. It was easier said than done. With a sigh, she typed out a reply. *Okay, but he is asking questions about why we were at Roman's Tavern the night we saw Jacob. What about your end?*

She sent the text and pulled out of the parking lot, heading toward the bookshop. She had been putting in extra hours since the time Lucian had tried to kill her to turn her into a hybrid. Originally, Darlene was furious with Maria for keeping the fact she was a werewolf a secret – an Exsul on top of that – but she understood more now why Maria did it. Darlene learned as much as she could about Exsuls in case Idris received that as his sentence. Plus working at the bookshop kept her busy, which meant no time for thinking about how she had killed Lucian.

No, do not go down that road, not right now. Darlene turned down the main street. She was almost at the bookshop. She would be busy soon.

If you enjoyed this sample then look for **Alpha Packed: A BBW Paranormal Shifter Romance - Book 2**.

Other Books by Darla Dunbar

- The Romeo Alpha BBW Paranormal Shifter Romance Series

- Romeo Alpha Blood Lines Romance Series

- The Alpha Feud BBW Paranormal Shifter Romance Series

- The Alpha Packed BBW Paranormal Shifter Romance Series

- The Daemon Paranormal Romance Chronicles

- The Leather Satchel Paranormal Romance Series

Get the latest update on new releases from the author at:

https://darladunbar.com/newsletter/

About the Author - Darla Dunbar

Darla has been interested in paranormal romance since she was a teenager in high school. It was then that she discovered she could fulfill her fantasies through her writing.

Observing people and human behavior in the area of romance has always been one of her favorite pastimes. Combining that with an overactive imagination is a sure fire way of coming up with interesting themes.

Connect with Darla Dunbar

I really appreciate you reading my book! Here are my social media coordinates:

Friend me on Facebook:
https://www.facebook.com/darladunbar/

Follow me on Twitter: https://twitter.com/DarlDunbar

Check me out on Goodreads:
https://www.goodreads.com/author/show/8425857.Darl
a_Dunbar

Subscribe to my newsletter:
https://darladunbar.com/newsletter/

Visit my website: https://darladunbar.com/

9 781987 863970